THE STORY OF BENTLEY BEAVER

by Marjorie Weinman Sharmat

Pictures by Lillian Hoban

An I CAN READ Book®

Harper & Row, Publishers

I Can Read Book is a registered trademark of
Harper & Row, Publishers, Inc.

The Story of Bentley Beaver
Text copyright © 1984 by Marjorie Weinman Sharmat
Illustrations copyright © 1984 by Lillian Hoban

Library of Congress Cataloging in Publication Data
Sharmat, Marjorie Weinman.
  The story of Bentley Beaver.

  (An I can read book)
  Summary: Bentley Beaver grows up, falls in love,
marries, has children and grandchildren, and dies
after a long and happy life.
  [1. Beavers—Fiction] I. Hoban, Lillian, ill.
II. Title. III. Series.
PZ7.S5299St 1984   [E]   82-47715
ISBN 0-06-025512-9
ISBN 0-06-025513-7 (lib. bdg.)

Designed by Al Cetta
1 2 3 4 5 6 7 8 9 10
First Edition

For Big Daddy,

who had a happy trip.

Bentley Beaver

was born on November fifth.

"We have a fine and fuzzy

baby beaver,"

said his mother.

"Hello, fine and fuzzy baby beaver,"

said his father.

"Let's name him Bentley."

"Bentley Beaver it is,"

said his mother.

Bentley's mother and father fed him
and played with him.
They talked to him
and sang to him.

One day Bentley Beaver said, "Mama."

One day he said, "Papa."

Many many days after that

he said, "Pentley Peaver."

"B is a hard letter to say,"

said his father.

Bentley's mother and father

gave him a present.

"Here are five sticks of wood,"

said his mother.

"Wood," said Bentley.

Bentley made a little house.

The house fell over.

Bentley made it again.

"Wood good," said Bentley.

Bentley got bigger.

His houses got bigger, too.

"Am I taller than my house?"

Bentley asked.

"You are the same,"

said his mother.

Bentley built a higher house.

"Am I taller than my house?"

he asked his father.

"You are getting taller, Bentley.

Your house is getting taller, too,"

said his father.

"I like being as tall as a house,"

said Bentley.

He built a few more houses

that were just as tall as he was.

One day Bentley Beaver started school.

He packed his book bag.

Then he unpacked it

and packed it again.

"Once was for practice,"

he told himself.

"Have a good day, Bentley Beaver,"

said his mother and father.

Bentley swung his book bag

back and forth.

He sang,

"Off to school, off to school.

Bentley Beaver's off to school."

He stopped singing.

"I don't want to be off to school.

I have never been off to school before.

What if it is not as much fun

as building houses?"

Then Bentley saw someone

down the path.

She was swinging a book bag, too.

"Hello," said Bentley.

"I am Bentley Beaver.

I am going to school,

and I am scared."

"Hello. I am Belinda Beaver.

I am going to school,

and I am scared, too."

"When I am scared, I sing,"

said Bentley.

"What a good idea," said Belinda.

Bentley and Belinda walked to school.

They sang,

"Off to school, off to school.

Off to school together."

Bentley and Belinda

did their homework together.

"How do you spell mud?"

asked Belinda.

"What is ten take away nine?"

asked Bentley.

Then they played on the swings.

They built houses

and other things from wood.

They built a little walk

between their houses.

Bentley Beaver was growing up.

He played the guitar

and ate a lot of potato chips.

"Soon you will be

all grown up,"

his mother said to him.

"I don't know if I will like

being grown up," said Bentley.

"I might be too busy

to play the guitar

and eat potato chips."

"What do you think

about being all grown up?"

Bentley asked Belinda.

"I don't know.

I am still growing," said Belinda.

"So am I," said Bentley,

"but I hope I will always have time

for singing."

"You will never be

too busy for that," said Belinda.

Bentley built higher and higher houses.

At last he was all grown up.

"My mother is a carpenter.

My father is a carpenter.

Now I am a carpenter, too," he said.

Bentley built and built.

"Wood feels good," he said.

"I can make wood stand up

or lie flat or slant.

I can make shapes with it."

Bentley picked up his guitar and sang,

"Oh, wood is good,

Wood is good.

It does much more

Than you'd think it could.

Wood is fun and sometimes splinters,

I like it in spring,

Summer, fall, and winter."

"I am in love,"

Bentley Beaver told himself.

Then he told a flower

and a bug

and a bird.

"There is someone else to tell,"

he said.

He told Belinda Beaver.

She already knew.

Bentley and Belinda got married.
Bentley's mother and father
played the piano at the wedding.
Then Bentley played the guitar
and sang.

"Now I am singing

because I am happy," said Bentley.

"Love is love is good,"

he sang.

"Love is even better than wood."

31

Bentley and Belinda built a house.

It took almost a year.

They built the first floor in spring,

the second floor in summer,

and the walk in fall.

"This house is much taller

than I am," said Bentley.

It was a strong and handsome house.

It had a room

just for singing.

Bentley and Belinda

were going to have a baby.

"We have never been a mother

or a father before,"

said Bentley.

"It is scary," said Belinda,

"like going to school

for the first time."

"I will write a song

for the baby," said Bentley.

"Do you think it will be

a boy or a girl?"

"It will be one or the other,"

said Belinda.

Bentley and Belinda had a boy.

They also had a girl.

They named the boy Fred,

and the girl Mary Ann.

Bentley wrote a new song.

"Two *baby beavers, fuzzy and nice,*

Belinda and I are lucky—twice."

"Mary Ann and Fred are fast growers,"
Bentley said to Belinda one day.
They gave each of the children
five sticks of wood.

Fred made a small piano.

Mary Ann made a candlestick.

They made up a song

called "Piano Meets Candlestick."

"That is a friendly song,"

said Bentley Beaver.

"We are a good and happy family,"

said Belinda.

"Yes, that is what we are,"

said Bentley.

Mary Ann and Fred

were growing up.

"Soon you will be

all grown up," Bentley said.

"What do you think about that?"

"I want to go to the city

and be a piano maker,"

said Fred.

"I want to go to the country

and be a candlestick maker,"

said Mary Ann.

One day Mary Ann and Fred

hugged and kissed

their mother and father good-bye.

"Not everyone wants

to stay by the lake

and be a carpenter,"

said Bentley Beaver.

Bentley and Belinda

missed their children.

"Let's make something

for Fred and Mary Ann," said Bentley.

He and Belinda

made two picture frames.

They sent one to Fred

and one to Mary Ann.

Fred sent back
a picture of himself
next to a piano.

Mary Ann sent back
a picture of herself
with a candlestick.

Bentley and Belinda

hung the pictures

in the singing room.

"Now our children have children,"

Bentley said to Belinda one day.

"Time is going by."

"What should we do about it?"

asked Belinda.

"First we could take a long trip,"

said Bentley.

"Then we can visit our children

and our children's children."

"Let's pack," said Belinda.

Bentley and Belinda took a trip

around the world.

They looked at many buildings.

"Nice, but not as nice

as our house," said Belinda.

"You and I are good builders."

"Yes, we are," said Bentley.

"Let's go teach our grandchildren

how to build a good house."

Bentley and Belinda

had six grandchildren.

Bentley helped each of them

build a small house

with five sticks of wood.

"Are you taller than your house

or is your house taller than you?"

he asked.

Then Bentley took out his guitar.

"Play a wood song, Grandpa."

Bentley and Belinda sang,

"Wood is good.

Wood is good.

It does much more

Than you'd think it could."

Their grandchildren sang, too.

Then Bentley and Belinda went home.

"Home," said Bentley Beaver.

"Home," said Belinda.

Bentley and Belinda grew old.

"I think we are very old,"

Bentley said to Belinda.

"I don't think we could be
much older," said Belinda.
Bentley started to sing.
"My life's been good,
Been good with wood,
My life's been good with you.
Some splinters, scrapes,
A few mistakes,
But I learned a thing or two."
"Are you singing
because you are scared
or because you are happy?"
asked Belinda.

"I am a little scared

and a little happy,"

said Bentley.

"Mostly I am happy,

because my life has been good.

It has been good

with my mother

and father.

It has been good

with you and the children.

It has been good with wood.

It has been good

in every way."

Bentley sang on,

"*I've told some tales,*

I've hammered nails,

I've had a happy trip.

When things went wrong,

I sang a song

And ate a potato chip."

On a windy day in spring

Bentley Beaver died.

"Good-bye, Bentley Beaver,"

said Belinda.

Bentley Beaver's children

and grandchildren

and great-grandchildren

live all over the world.

Now and then

they speak of him.

They say he was funny and kind.

They speak of how much

he loved wood.

They talk about his guitar

and how much he liked singing.

The details

have become fuzzy with time.

But no one will ever forget

Bentley Beaver.

BENTLEY'S SONG

My life's been good,

Been good with wood,

My life's been good with you.

Some splin-ters, scrapes,

A few mis-takes,

But I learned a thing or two.

I've told some tales,

I've ham—mered nails,

I've had a hap—py trip.

When things went wrong,

I sang a song

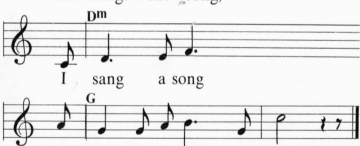

And ate a po-ta - to chip.